The Flopsy Bunnies

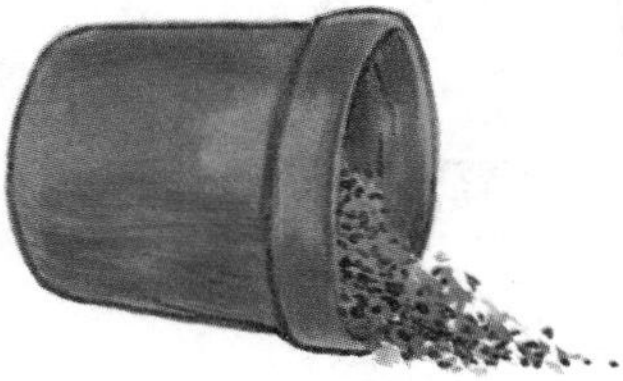

Retold by
Sarah Toast

Cover illustrated by
Anita Nelson

Book illustrated by
Pat Schoonover

Based on the original story by Beatrix Potter with all new illustrations.

Manufactured in U.S.A.

8 7 6 5 4 3 2 1

ISBN: 0-7853-2201-9

PUBLICATIONS INTERNATIONAL, LTD.

Benjamin and Flopsy Bunny had a very large, cheerful family. Their many children were called the Flopsy Bunnies so no one had to remember all their names.

Sometimes, when there was not quite enough to eat, Benjamin would borrow cabbage from Flopsy's brother, Peter Rabbit. But sometimes Peter Rabbit had no cabbage to spare. When this happened, the Flopsy Bunnies set off across the field to the trash heap outside Mr. McGregor's garden.

One day, to their great joy, Benjamin and the little bunnies found lots of overgrown lettuce in the trash heap. The bunnies stuffed themselves, which made them very sleepy.

The bunnies lay down in a pile of grass clippings to sleep. Before he nodded off, Benjamin put a paper bag over his head to keep off the flies.

The little Flopsy Bunnies slept soundly in the sun, but a small mouse rustled across the paper bag and woke up Benjamin Bunny.

Thomasina Tittlemouse was apologizing to Benjamin when the two heard heavy footsteps approaching. Suddenly, Mr. McGregor dumped grass clippings on top of the bunnies!

Benjamin slid under the paper bag, and Thomasina jumped into a jam jar. The Flopsy Bunnies smiled in their sleep, dreaming that their mother was tucking them into bed.

Mr. McGregor looked down and saw some funny little brown things sticking up through the clippings.

A fly settled on one of the little brown things and it twitched.

Mr. McGregor climbed down onto the trash heap. "One, two, three, four, five, six little rabbits!" he counted as he dropped them into a sack.

The Flopsy Bunnies smiled in their sleep, dreaming that their mother was turning them in bed. They were still so sleepy from eating the lettuce that they didn't even wake up when Mr. McGregor tied up the sack and left it on the wall.

Mr. McGregor went to the toolshed to put away the lawn mower. While Mr. McGregor wasn't around, Mrs. Flopsy Bunny came across the field. She was looking for Benjamin and her little bunnies.

Flopsy looked suspiciously at the sack on the wall. Then she heard noises from the trash heap.

The mouse came out of the jam jar, and Benjamin took the paper bag off his head. They had a very sad story to tell Flopsy.

Flopsy Bunny tried to untie the string on the sack, but she could not. Benjamin Bunny tried to pick up the sack to carry it home, but he could not. The two rabbits were in despair.

Thomasina Tittlemouse was a very clever little mouse, however. She nibbled a hole in the bottom corner of the sack.

Benjamin and Flopsy reached into the sack and pulled out the little bunnies. The Flopsy Bunnies finally began to wake up.

While all the little rabbits yawned and shook off sleep, Benjamin and Flopsy stuffed the empty sack with rotten squash, two decayed turnips, and an old polishing brush. Then they all hid under a bush and looked out for Mr. McGregor.

Mr. McGregor came back for the sack. He picked it up and carried it as if it were rather heavy.

The Flopsy bunnies followed at a comfortable distance, wanting to see what Mr. McGregor would do.

The bunnies all watched as Mr. McGregor went inside. They crept to the window to listen. The youngest Flopsy Bunny got on the windowsill.

Mr. McGregor said to his wife, “One, two, three, four, five, six little rabbits!”

“What have they spoiled now?” asked Mrs. McGregor.

“I have six rabbits for supper!” said Mr. McGregor.

“I shall use the skins to line my old coat!” said Mrs. McGregor.

Mrs. McGregor untied the sack and reached in. When she felt the vegetables, she became very angry. She thought Mr. McGregor had tricked her on purpose.

Mr. McGregor was very angry too. He was so upset that he threw a squash right out the window and knocked the youngest Flopsy Bunny clear off the windowsill.

Benjamin and Flopsy Bunny thought that it was time to go home. Flopsy carried her youngest bunny.

The next Christmas morning, Thomasina Tittlemouse got a lovely present from the Flopsy Bunnies. They gave her enough rabbit hair to make a coat with a hood, a handsome muff, and a pair of warm mittens.